W9-AVT-337

Cheers for 20 Years
with *The Adirondack Kids*®

"For two decades I've had the pleasure of reading the VanRipers' *The Adirondack Kids*® series—first as a book reviewer for *Adirondack Life* magazine and later as a mother, sharing The Adirondack Kids' adventures with my own children. Book after book the VanRipers have shown the next generation what it is that makes the Adirondack Park so special— our protected landscape, with its lakes, peaks and ponds, and the gift that it is to explore and enjoy it with friends and family. Happy 20th, Gary, Carol and Justin!

—**Annie Stoltie**, Editor, *Adirondack Life* magazine

"Mixing action, humor, mystery and a whole lot of the great outdoors, *The Adirondack Kids*® shows off the best of regional fiction. If you are from the Adirondacks, you'll be thrilled to see places, people, and animals that hit close to home. If you live in a city, well, here is your doorway into a world of bears, huge fish, skunks, eagles, and moose, with some bad guys, local legends, and buried treasure to boot. Quick reads and fast-moving stories from a land that was made just for kids."

—The late **Michael Sullivan**, author of *Raising Boy Readers*; *Connecting Boys with Books*; *What Libraries Can Do* and *Connecting Boys with Books 2*, *Closing the Reading Gap* all for the American Library Association. See also the *Escapade Johnson* series for young readers.

"Mountain-high congratulations to Gary and Justin VanRiper on the twentieth anniversary of the *Adirondack Kids*® series. The adventure-packed volumes have introduced many, many kids to the great outdoors— and also into the pages of many, many good books!

High-interest and engaging, each volume in the Series welcomes kids on an exciting new journey set within the outdoor landscape—mountains, lakes, shores, and more. The series is also smartly written with built-in authentic learning masterfully woven into the action-packed storyline.

I have personally witnessed hundreds of students gain joy and excitement from the series. They have provided a tremendous treat to our children!"

—**Sandra K. Athans**, Literacy Specialist, Children's Writer, and Advisor for the West Central Upstate NY Region of the Society of Children's Book Writers and Illustrators (SCBWI).

The Adirondack Kids®
Justin & Gary VanRiper
Copyright © 2020. All rights reserved.

First Paperback Printing, June 2020

The Adirondack Kids® Series

The Adirondack Kids® is a registered trademark
of Adirondack Kids Press, Ltd.
Original First Volume Self-Published in 2001.
Self-published one new volume a year
for 20 consecutive years.

More than 160,000 copies in the series sold to date.
Celebrated 20th Anniversary for series
in 2020 with release of a revised and expanded 20th
Anniversary Edition of Volume #1

Volume #5 won Adirondack Center for Writing
Literary Award in 2004–5 for Best Children's Book

The Adirondack Kids®

Volumes 1–10: Chronicles a Summer
Volumes 11–13: Chronicles Autumn, Winter & Spring
Volumes 14–18: Back to Summer
Volumes 19 & 20: Back to Autumn

All rights reserved. No part of this publication
may be reproduced, stored in a retrieval system, or
transmitted in any form or by any means –
electronic, mechanical, photocopying, recording,
or otherwise – without the prior, written
permission of the publisher and copyright owners.

Published by
Adirondack Kids Press, Ltd.
39 Second Street
Camden, New York 13316

Printed in the United States of America
by Patterson Printing, Michigan
Graphic Design by Nancy Did It!
Illustrated by Susan Loeffler and Glenn Guy

ISBN 978-1-7346509-0-7

The
Adirondack
Kids®

Justin & Gary VanRiper
Illustrations by Glenn Guy

Adirondack Kids Press
Camden, New York

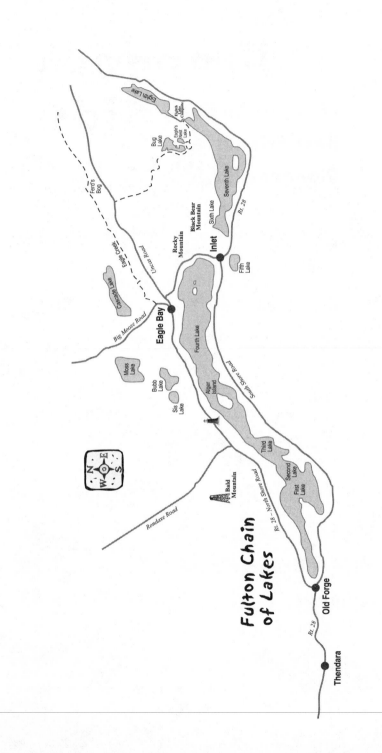

Contents

Dedication

*When we first met and dared to introduce
Justin & Jackie & Nick & Dax to the vast and
wonderful world of books, we had no idea
if anyone else would want to get to know and
spend any time with them.*

*How humbled and thankful and thrilled we are
that so many young people have welcomed
our characters into their hearts and camps and
become their friends – hiking, paddling,
swimming, horseback riding, biking, boating,
skating, caving, birding, fishing
and eating 'smores around the campfire.*

*To you, all of our wonderful readers,
real Adirondack Kids, who have set down your
electronic devices to get out and explore
the great outdoors.*

Gary & Carol & Justin
June, 2020

chapter one

"Bearly" To Camp

Justin Robert sat in the back seat of the jeep staring down at his sneakers resting firmly on the carpet. It had just occurred to him that this was the first summer he could sit up normally and make both of his feet touch the floor.

"Here you go, Son," said Mr. Robert. "Soft chocolate with chocolate sprinkles, right?"

It was a family tradition. Stop for ice cream at the Pied Piper in Old Forge before traveling the last few miles to camp.

"Thanks, Dad." He took the cone and shifted uneasily in his seat. "Can we get going now?"

"What's the big hurry?" asked Mrs. Robert.

"I don't know," Justin said. But he did know. He hadn't seen his best friends for months. Eight to be exact. And while they had talked on the phone a few times, it wasn't the same thing as hanging out together.

They were interrupted by a cry from someone waiting in line at the Piper for a burger. Everyone standing in the parking lot turned first to the lady making

the commotion and then followed her finger point-
ing to the highway. People began scurrying for their
cars like a crowd caught by surprise in a sudden
downpour of rain.

Justin scrambled to his knees and turned to peer
out the rear window of the jeep. He pulled the brim
of his bucket hat away from his eyes for a better look.

A long line of traffic in both lanes was at a full
stop as a huge black bear lumbered leisurely down
the middle of the road.

"He acts like he owns the place," Justin said.
"Let's get out and watch him." He reached for the
door handle.

"Sit right where you are, young man," Mrs. Robert
said. His mom always said *young man* when she
expected unquestioned obedience. "We will wait
right here until he passes by."

"Caution and respect," Mr. Robert reminded him.
"You know how unpredictable a wild animal can be."

I think he's coming this way," Justin said, his eyes
widening.

His dad was right. The bear had suddenly turned and
was walking in a direct path toward the Roberts' jeep.

"Roll up the windows, *now*," said Mr. Robert, firmly.

All three hundred and fifty pounds of black bear
moved forward on four stocky legs with a purpose.
The huge creature was preoccupied with a tall cylin-
drical can, filled with discarded portions of burgers
and fries, that stood near the front of the jeep.

Justin's heart started pounding. He liked computers,

...a huge black bear lumbered leisurely
down the middle of the road...

3

biking and peanut butter cups. But his passion was animals.

"Awesome," he whispered as the bear's body brushed against his window. Then it stood up directly in front of the Roberts' vehicle to attack the container. Only its wide black back showed through the windshield, and for a moment it appeared as if it might sit down using the hood of the jeep as a seat.

The can tipped over with a sharp clang spilling its contents onto the pavement. The top fell spinning and rolled away. The bear began pawing through the debris.

"Many of the local bears are used to finding a meal in garbage," Mr. Robert explained. "Since the dump closed they are even wandering into campsites and –"

"Oh my!" Mrs. Robert exclaimed.

Justin and his dad laughed as she held up a cone in a fist dripping with melted strawberry ice cream that was littered with rainbow sprinkles.

"Don't laugh at me," she said. "Look at yourselves."

All three had their favorite flavor streaming down from their cones, the sticky treat beginning to trickle over their fingers.

They never noticed the bear slowly drift away as they shared napkins to clean their hands.

Traffic returned to normal and hungry tourists began to line up again at the Pied Piper's take-out window.

"Are we ready to head for camp?" Mr. Robert asked.

"Absolutely," answered Justin, excitedly.

Summer vacation had hardly begun and he already had an adventure to share with his friends.

chapter two

Best Friends

Justin was still licking his sticky hand when the Roberts pulled into their driveway. It was very steep and at places seemed to drop straight down, but the jeep's all-wheel drive handled the descent with ease.

They all slightly held their breath the first time down the hill each new season. Everyone remembered the year the brakes gave out and the old station wagon rolled out of control and into the camp's main bedroom below. Justin was only four at the time, but even he could recall that short and terrifying ride.

"Well, here we are," said Mr. Robert, the way he had said it every summer Justin could remember. The ten-year-old loved his family. He loved the traditions. And he loved camp.

"Whoa, slow down there young man," called his mother as he bolted out of the vehicle and headed for the path leading to the neighbor's camp.

Justin helped unload the jeep. He scooped up his worn out copy of *Robin Hood,* action figures and game cartridges which were strewn all over the back seat.

"And don't forget your pillow," Mrs. Robert reminded him.

The fresh mountain air reached deep down inside his body. The bittersweet aroma of the pine trees always acted to erase ties to back home almost immediately.

The Roberts' camp was situated on the north shore of Fourth Lake, one of eight lakes along what was called the Fulton Chain of Lakes. Justin's great grandfather built the camp before there was even a road to the spot. Original building materials had been delivered by boat up the chain and for three generations not much about the camp's structure had changed.

"Can I sleep on the porch?" Justin asked.

"Of course you can," said Mrs. Robert.

The *sleeping porch* they called it, and it was Justin's favorite place to spend summer nights, unless there were thunder and lightning. Then Mom and Dad's room was the place to be.

The porch was upstairs, enclosed with large windows all around and had a commanding view of the lake. Justin began putting his clothes into the dresser drawers and sneezed. The whole room smelled of moth balls. His mom said it kept the mice away all winter.

"Justin, there's someone here to see you," Mrs. Robert called.

It's got to be Nick, he thought and ran headlong down the stairs.

"Hi, Justin," said a girl's voice as he stormed into the living room.

"Hey," Justin said. It was a reserved response, but he really was happy to see her. Jackie Salsberry was twelve years old and one of his best friends. She collected rocks, put worms on hooks and wasn't afraid of salamanders or snakes, but after all, she was a girl. Hugging her was definitely out of the question.

"Dad let me bring the putt-putt," said Jackie and smiled. The Salsberrys lived summers on a small island just off the center of the lake and slightly east of the Roberts' camp. It was the first year the aluminum row boat with small outboard engine became her very own lake transportation. "I saw your jeep pull in. Have you seen Nick yet?"

"Can I go now, Mom?" called Justin. The rustle of paper grocery bags and the clatter of dishes and pans betrayed her presence in the kitchen.

"Yes –" she said. The screen door banged shut before his mother finished her sentence.

The short winding path between the Roberts' and Barnes' camps was well worn. The exposed tangle of tree roots jutting upward along the uneven ground could easily trip anyone not familiar with the way. But for Justin and Jackie they provided places to plant their sneakers and push off, helping them to run along even faster.

"Hey you guys, up here." It was Nick Barnes, calling from the woods.

Justin and Jackie turned abruptly and rambled up a slight incline where their friend stood in the midst of a small clearing, his hands on his hips.

Two months younger than Justin, Nick was still a bit bigger and much louder. "Look at this mess," he said.

Pioneer Village was located in the thin woods between the boys' two camps. A mass of long and short sticks lay scattered about the forest floor.

"Where's the village hall?" Jackie asked. "And the general store?"

"Everything's gone," Justin said. "Even the pots and pans."

"We've got a lot of work to do," said Nick.

Winter had indeed taken its toll.

chapter three

Pioneer Village

No grown-ups allowed! There wasn't a sign up, but that was one of the unwritten rules of Pioneer Village. Every summer one of the first things the three friends did was to survey the damage done to their forest community. Then they would rebuild the walls and hold elections. Pioneer Village had a mayor, several retail shoppes and even a hospital.

It was late afternoon the day following their reunion when Justin, Jackie and Nick met again at the center of town.

"There are plenty of sticks left," Justin said. "Let's fix our houses first."

The residents started by constructing their own homes, but it didn't really matter. As the summer wore on and they played games of Pioneer Village, they would trade houses and take on different roles.

"It looks like there are even more branches than last year," noted Nick. He was busy making piles of building supplies. "The village will be great this year."

The three friends set to work on the buildings. Each selected their own small site and began by outlining a space with stacks of sticks. It didn't take long to shape a structure because the walls for each one were only a few feet high and there were no roofs. The thick forest canopy high overhead kept out all but the heaviest of rains.

"I found a pan," said Jackie. It lay on the ground half covered with brown pine needles.

By dusk a few more items had been recovered – a rusty tea pot, two plastic cups and several forks and spoons. The general store was rebuilt and partially stocked with the items found.

"It's time for a meeting," Justin said.

"And then dinner," said Nick. "I'm hungry."

The friends gathered at a large boulder in the village. It was a place much higher up the slope and the climb was steep enough to require walking sticks to assist them in the ascent. They called the place *The Rock* and it overlooked all of Pioneer Village. A sliver of lake was visible from there through a slight break in the tree cover.

An Eastern Chipmunk greeted them atop the boulder at the meeting place. It sat up on its hind legs, scolded the intruders and quickly darted away. They sat down facing one another.

"I call the meeting to order," said Jackie. She was the oldest and the boys had no trouble with her getting things started. "Do I have a nomination for mayor?"

"Yes," answered Nick, quickly.

"Okay, who is it?" she asked.

"Me!" Nick said.

Nick nominated himself every year, and had been mayor as long as they could remember playing.

"Do you care, Justin?" Jackie asked.

"No," said Justin. He really preferred to be the shopkeeper or banker whenever he could and collect everyone's money anyway.

"All in favor?" she asked. It was unanimous. Nick was mayor and led the rest of the meeting. Justin was chosen to run the general store and Jackie to operate the bait shop and hospital.

"We should try to find some more things before we go home for dinner," Justin suggested. He wanted a few more objects in his store to sell. "Let's keep looking around."

They met with little success finding only a broken bottle and another plastic cup.

"Mom wondered where all these went last summer," said Nick, tossing the cup into the general store. Then he noticed the shopkeeper was missing. "Hey, where's Justin?"

"Over here," Justin called. He had found the crude wooden sign shaped like an arrow with the words **Pioneer Village** carved roughly on one side. It was nailed to a thin wooden stake.

"Let's put it back up," said Jackie. "That will make things official."

Justin nodded and picked up a stone to pound the sign back into the ground.

WHACK – WHACK – WHACK – SNAP!

The tip of the sign post splintered off and away.

Justin picked up a stone to pound
the sign back into the ground.

"Hey, I hit something," exclaimed Justin.

"It's probably just another dumb old rock," said Nick. "They're all over around here."

"I don't think so," Justin said. "It didn't feel like a rock." He put the sign down and began to scoop the soft dark earth with his hands.

Jackie ran back to the general store. "I'll get the spoons," she said.

"You have to pay for those!" Justin called after her.

They didn't dig long before metal hit metal. Nick's spoon tapped against the surface of an object only three to four inches below the forest floor.

"What is it?" Jackie asked.

"It looks like a small box," Justin said, excitedly. "I think we found buried treasure!"

chapter four

Buried Treasure

The box wasn't big. It just seemed big.

"When does this thing end?" complained Nick as six hands continued to scoop black dirt away looking for the edges of the covered container.

"Watch for worms," urged Jackie as they dug. "I want to go fishing tonight."

It seemed to take forever, but in just a few minutes the box was pulled out onto the ground.

"How will we open it?" asked Nick. "We don't have a key. Maybe we'll have to get some dynamite or something and blow it open!"

"It's not locked," said Justin. It was true. The box was held shut by a small latch, rusted from the time spent underground.

"I wonder if pirates left it," continued Nick. "It might have gold coins and crystals and diamonds and stuff in it – maybe even an eye patch."

"Let's open it," suggested Jackie.

"Since I am the mayor, I think I should open it," said Nick, using his most grown up tone of voice. He reached out for the box.

"No," said Jackie. "Justin found it. I think he should have the honor."

Nick shrugged. "Ah, there's probably nothing in it but a bunch of big old creepy bugs anyway," he said.

All three sat cross-legged in a small circle around the hole in the ground. Justin set the box onto his lap and worked the latch. It was stubborn at first, but suddenly gave way. He lightly brushed off the top one more time and opened the lid wide.

"It's a tackle box," said Jackie.

Inside and near the top was a small metal tray with more than a dozen compartments. Three of the spaces held small and colorful wooden fishing lures, their big eyes staring up at them.

"Is there any gold?" asked Nick. He still hoped pirates were in some way involved in the adventure.

Justin slowly lifted the tray. At the bottom of the box lay a wooden toy soldier, a small silver coin and wrapped in plastic, an old comic book.

Adirondack Sky Pilot, said Nick, reading the title on the comic. "Who's that?" The cover showed a wild, wide-eyed pilot at the controls of a plane gritting his teeth. The book appeared in near perfect condition.

"Look at this coin," mused Jackie. She turned it over. "It looks like a nickel, but it has a buffalo on one side and a Native American on the other side."

"I thought maybe it was from another country," said Justin.

"I'll bet we're rich," said Nick. He couldn't get the idea of treasure out of his head. "I'll bet some pirate stole it and sailed up from Old Forge and buried it right here."

"This soldier looks kind of cool," said Justin. He turned it over and over in his fingers examining it closely. "It doesn't bend like my other action guys, and the paint is almost all off it, but I still think it's cool."

"What will we do with this stuff?" asked Nick. "Let's shoot odds and evens for it."

Once again it was Jackie who offered the most sensible course of action. "I think we should take it over to Justin's camp," she said. "Since it's on his family's property, maybe his mom or dad even knows something about how it got here."

"Do you think your grandfather was a pirate?" asked Nick, hopefully.

"Yeah, right," answered Justin. "He was a mean, scary old pirate who went fishing, read comic books and played with toy soldiers!"

chapter five

Self Sacrifice

The early evening light was reflecting off the lake when the three Pioneer Villagers hurried up the camp steps. Mr. and Mrs. Robert were relaxing in their Adirondack chairs on the front porch enjoying the easy breeze. Justin led the way cradling the mystery box under his right arm.

"What's that you have there, Justin?" asked Mr. Robert. "It looks like an old tackle box."

Justin frowned. "How do you know what it is?" he asked, disappointed he couldn't amaze his parents with their discovery.

"Just a wild guess," he said and winked at Mrs. Robert. She smiled back.

"Was your father a pirate?" asked Nick.

"Was he a *what*?" asked Mr. Robert.

Justin interrupted. "Never mind, Dad. We found this old box buried at Pioneer Village. Just look at what's inside!"

The latch was loose now and the box opened easily. Justin carefully emptied the contents onto a small table between his parents' two chairs.

"Hmmm," said Mr. Robert picking up one of the old lures. "I'd nearly forgotten about this old box."

"You mean you know about it!" Justin said, surprised.

"I should," Mr. Robert said. He smiled. "I put it there."

Mr. Robert explained that when he was a boy a little older than Justin, he thought it would be fun to put a few of his favorite things into a container and bury it where someone might find it years later. The comic and coin were his. The wooden soldier and fishing lures were his father's. They buried the treasure together.

"You were right, Dad, it was a great idea," said Justin. "You wouldn't believe how excited we were when we found it."

Nick sounded let down. "Well, it was kind of neat," he said. "But there weren't any diamonds or gold."

"Maybe you could make a little time capsule of your own," suggested Mrs. Robert.

"What do you mean, Mom?" asked Justin.

"She means you three should bury a treasure that one of your own children might find some day," explained Mr. Robert.

Nick perked up. "Yeah," he said. "I've got a bunch of old junk I don't want any more. My mom said if I don't throw it out, she will."

"Not junk," said Mr. Robert. "Something special. Justin's grandpa and I fished with these lures." He held one up. Hooks seemed to dangle everywhere from its short pudgy body. "They don't make them like this anymore."

"What about the coin and the soldier?" asked Justin.

"And the comic?" asked Jackie.

"Well, the Buffalo nickel and the comic were from collections I had started when I was a bit younger than Justin," said Mr. Robert.

"You mean before you were big and strong like I am now, right Dad?" Justin said. He puffed his chest out and held his head a little higher when he said it.

"That's right, Son," said Mr. Robert.

"What about the wooden soldier?" asked Nick.

"The wooden soldier...." Mr. Robert made direct eye contact with Nick. "I think the wooden soldier was hand carved by one of my father's ancestors. Why, he might have even been..."

"A pirate, yes!" exclaimed Nick as he jumped and clenched both of his fists.

Mr. Robert laughed. "You never know."

"Usually those who find a treasure have to divide it," said Mrs. Robert. "We'll leave you three alone to decide what to do with your discovery."

The two stood up and started down the steps hand in hand toward the lake.

"Don't take too long, Justin," his mom called back to him. "Dinner's very soon. And remember, you and your father are getting up early in the morning."

The three friends stood looking down at the items on the table.

"It's up to you, Justin," said Jackie. "I feel funny

taking any of your dad's great things."

"What do you mean?" asked Nick as he moved his head from side to side studying the fishing lures with the popping eyes. It seemed no matter where he moved, their gaze followed him. "His dad couldn't have cared that much. He stuck the stuff in the ground and forgot about it."

This wasn't easy for Justin. Sharing was not one of his strengths. Since turning ten a month earlier his mom had said she expected him to start acting a lot more grown up.

"There are three lures," reasoned Justin out loud. "We could each have one of them. And the other things, well, you go ahead and pick first, Jackie. Then Nick, then me."

"Are you sure, Justin?" Jackie asked.

"Yes, positive," Justin said. Actually, he loved the wooden soldier and thought the nickel was cool even though it wasn't from another country. It was really hard, but he thought letting his friends go first was the right thing to do.

"I've got to have the soldier carved by the pirate," said Nick.

Jackie chose the coin. "I'm going to learn more about this nickel," she said.

"Great," said Justin weakly, but managed a slight smile. "I get the comic."

chapter six

Moss Lake

5 a.m. came quickly.

It was still dark when Justin's father woke him from a deep sleep. He shot straight up in bed with his eyes open wide. This was a morning his father had promised him for a long time. They were going to paddle a kayak in Moss Lake and look for loons.

Everything was made ready the night before. A brand new two-seat kayak was safely strapped onto the top of the jeep. The camera equipment was on the back seat packed in a small watertight case.

Justin carried two small bags of GORP (a mix of granola, oatmeal, raisins and peanuts) and two small bottles of water in a vest his dad had bought him for what he anticipated would be many such day trips. Or, as in this case, a half-day trip. Underneath, he wore a sweatshirt and under that a t-shirt – layers of clothing that could be peeled off as the day grew warmer.

"Life preservers in the back, Justin?" asked Mr. Robert as the two climbed into the jeep.

"Yes, and so's the paddle," answered Justin. He had stopped yawning and rubbing his eyes the minute they walked outdoors.

The air was chilly, the fog was thick and the windshield was wet. It was early summer in the Adirondacks, but father and son could still see their own steamy breath when they talked.

The drive to Moss Lake took less than fifteen minutes. There were no other vehicles in the parking lot.

"We may have the whole lake to ourselves this morning," said Mr. Robert. There was a cry from somewhere deep out in the fog. "Well, almost all to ourselves." Justin managed a sheepish grin.

A poster with black-and-white print and a drawing of a loon was tacked to the registry at the trail head where the two signed in. The headline read in large bold capital letters:

HELP PROTECT LOONS

LOONS, THEIR CHICKS AND NEST SITES ARE PROTECTED BY NEW YORK STATE AND FEDERAL LAW

Below the headline was a short list of rules to follow when observing the birds.

"Disturbance of loons during the nesting season may lead to nest abandonment," Justin read out loud.

"What does *abandonment* mean, Dad?"

"Well, that means if someone gets too close to loons when they have their nests, the parents might leave and never come back," explained Mr. Robert.

"Let's not get too close if we ever see one, Dad," urged Justin. "I don't want the loon eggs to be left all alone without the mom to keep them warm."

He went on to the next rule.

"Do not drive loons away from sheltered areas into open water where boat traffic is heavy," he read and then finished the short list. "Please respect and enjoy this symbol of the wilderness by staying as far away from them as possible."

"That's why we brought our binoculars and tele-photo camera lens," said Mr. Robert. "If we happen to see loons this morning, I have no intention of moving us too close to them."

"They must be pretty special birds to have posters made for them," Justin said.

"Well, there are some two thousand loons in the Adirondacks," explained Mr. Robert. "But they are still a bird species of special concern and need our protection and care."

Justin didn't need convincing. He loved all animals and thought some day he might even have a job taking care of them.

A short path led from the parking lot to the shore-line of the lake where fresh bear prints were pressed into the wet sand. Wildlife took turns breaking the silence as they eased the kayak into the water.

Rat-tat-tat-tat, a woodpecker's hammering sounded through the trees.

K-chee-k-chee-k-chee-k-chee, a young Osprey cried out from the small island located at the center of the small lake.

Justin climbed into the front seat of the boat. "I'll paddle so you can take pictures, okay Dad?" he said. Taking hold of the long paddle and grasping it in the middle, he dipped the blade at one end gently into the water, then slowly the other. It was awkward at first and he banged the side of the boat a few times as he sought the right grip. The kayak inched forward. Neither spoke as the vessel slowly moved through the fog.

"We're not lost," Mr. Robert softly whispered reassuringly.

How does Dad know what I'm thinking? thought Justin.

Fog was everywhere and the young navigator had no idea where they were headed. The water was silver and flat, like a mirror. It felt to Justin at times as if they were suspended in the air where there were no boundaries above, to the side or below. His dad's comforting words helped him to relax and simply enjoy the sensation.

K-chee, k-chee, the Osprey cried again, but sounded much closer this time. The ghostly silhouette of a Tamarack tree began to appear, and then another and another. Justin shivered and wasn't sure if it was caused by the chilly morning air, or the eerie shapes looming just ahead. The form of a large bird appeared, perched at the end of a crooked branch. On a larger limb just above it was a mass of sticks.

K-chee-k-chee-k-chee. The cry came not from the bird they could see, but from the large tangle of sticks over its head.

"That's the Osprey's nest, Son."

"Is that the baby in the nest?" Justin whispered.

"Yes," answered Mr. Robert, softly. "And he's hungry."

Another ghostly form suddenly soared into view as a second adult Osprey arrived clutching a fish in its talons.

"Breakfast!" whispered Justin, excitedly. "Where are the binoculars, Dad?"

"Take a look through the camera lens," Mr. Robert offered.

Justin pointed the camera with its long heavy lens upward. He could see the adult bird in greater detail perched on the edge of the nest.

"This is so cool," whispered Justin. "I can see the fish and the baby's beak and everything."

Suddenly a resounding wail cut through the hush, like a wolf howling. It seemed to echo everywhere.

Justin recalled hearing that sound from a distance for the first time on Fourth Lake late last summer. It was somewhat familiar, but still gave him goose bumps, especially when it sounded so close and he was surrounded on every side by the fog.

"Let's paddle to the other side of the island," whispered Mr. Robert.

chapter seven

On the Wild's Side

Justin had heard his dad talk a lot about Common Loons, and was familiar with what they looked like because images of the popular bird seemed to be everywhere in the Adirondacks.

Studying the photographs his dad had taken for magazines, he knew the birds were black and white with black-and-white checkered backs and were about the size of a goose. And he loved that they had red eyes. He had once seen a stuffed loon at the Old Forge Hardware store propped up on a shelf in the book section, but had never seen a real one. He understood it had been a long time since a pair had been spotted on his lake at camp because it was so busy with motorboats.

Coached by his father, Justin wasn't knocking the side of the boat with the paddle as often now and managed to maneuver the kayak quietly and slowly around the perimeter of the island. The solid white blanket of fog began to separate. There were bigger and bigger gaps between the wisps of mist and Justin could see further out in front of him.

"Let's move away from the island now," Mr. Robert said. "The loons on this lake may already have a nest here and we don't want to scare them." The island slowly disappeared behind.

Then between dips of the paddle blade into the water an adult Common Loon suddenly appeared at the surface, emerging like a submarine from the depths of the sea. It was only a few feet in front of the kayak and was paddling swiftly and effortlessly directly across their path. It was so close Justin could see beads of water trailing down its head and neck.

"Don't move, just watch," Justin heard his dad whisper.

No problem. He was frozen in place. In seconds the bird was gone, swallowed up by the fog, and Justin began to breathe again.

Who scared who?" Justin said. He was stunned, but happy. He was beginning to understand why his dad loved the wilderness enough to write about it and take so many pictures.

"I am so glad we were able to experience that together," said Mr. Robert as he leaned forward and rubbed Justin's shoulder. "Now you have photographs in your mind you'll have forever."

"Wait until I tell Nick and Jackie!" said Justin. "They won't believe it!"

In a few hours the fog had lifted away completely. Warm bright light moved across the western shoreline and the only clouds now were high in a deep blue and turquoise sky.

A Common Loon suddenly appeared at the surface,
emerging like a submarine from the depths of the sea.

The lake doesn't seem quite so large when you can see it all at once, thought Justin. The two paddlers saw a white-tailed deer stooping for a drink and a noisy Belted Kingfisher that was chattering as it flew back and forth from shoreline to island several times. A small breeze began to create ripples that moved across the entire face of the water.

Their GORP was gone as they approached the spot where they had entered the lake four hours earlier. A beaver poked its head up out of the water, saw the kayak, slapped its tail and disappeared.

Justin was startled and blinked his eyes as water sprayed nearly a foot into the air and fell alongside and into their vessel.

The bottom of the boat finally came to a grinding stop in the gritty sand at shore.

Father and son had not talked much all morning. They had mainly just watched and listened.

A man and a woman rambled down the trail and set their bright yellow canoe into the lake as Justin and his dad pulled their kayak out.

"See anything interesting out there?" asked the man in a loud voice.

"Oh, a couple of things," said Mr. Robert. He and Justin simply looked at each other and smiled.

chapter eight

Loons on Fourth Lake

The early morning adventure with his dad at Moss Lake tired Justin out. Early afternoon felt like early evening and he was happy just to sit on the family dock with Nick and Jackie, fishing poles in the water. His friends listened as he described his experience.

"Loons can even stay underwater for up to five minutes when they dive," explained Justin, proud of his newly acquired knowledge.

Nick shrugged. "So what?" he said. "That's not so long. I'll bet I can hold my breath for *six* minutes."

"You couldn't hold your breath for six *seconds*," argued Justin.

"I can too," Nick shot back.

"No way," said Justin. "You couldn't stop talking that long. Besides, loons don't just hold their breath when they're under the water. They're swimming really fast and chasing fish around."

"We can settle this right now," interrupted Jackie. "I have a watch on with a second hand."

The boys really admired Jackie's watch and wanted one, too. It was a regular watch and a stop watch all in one. It was waterproof, shock proof and most importantly, Jackie-proof. No one really knew what all the extra buttons were for, but they would also glow in the dark making the timepiece look most impressive day or night.

"Okay Mr. 'I Can Hold My Breath For *Six* Minutes', get ready," Jackie said sharply.

"Set."

She pressed one of the glow-in-the-dark buttons. "Go!"

Nick breathed in deeply until his eyes slightly crossed and his chest heaved out.

Jackie sat motionless on the dock staring at the watch. Justin sat staring at Nick, who after only about fifteen seconds was already turning a reddish color in his cheeks.

"It hasn't been twenty seconds yet," announced Jackie to let Nick know how he was doing.

This news discouraged Nick, who was now blinking rapidly and slowly allowing air to escape from his pressed lips.

"It's still not fair," complained Justin. "He should start moving his legs around or something, like he's a loon chasing a fish."

Justin demonstrated by laying with his back on the dock flailing his arms and kicking wildly.

"Thirty seconds," said Jackie, and with that a gush of air burst from Nick's mouth followed by a deep and desperate inhale of fresh mountain oxygen.

"No fair," said Nick, as he gasped for air. "Justin tried to make me laugh kicking his legs around like that. I get to try again."

As the two were arguing, the tip of Nick's abandoned pole began to wiggle. Then it wiggled fast. Then it bent straight over and the entire pole began to skid across the dock.

"Hey, Nick," said Justin.

"So, are you going to let me try again?" asked his stubborn friend.

"Yeah," answered Justin. "This time you can do it for real."

He pointed to Nick's fishing rod about to slip off the dock.

"You can dive for a fish – and your pole!"

Nick made an admirable but useless lunge at the rod as it toppled over the end of the dock and splashed into the lake.

Nick, Jackie and Justin dropped on their knees and peered down into the clear water.

"Isn't it amazing how things look bigger under the water than they really are?" Jackie said. A glint of sunlight reflected off the giant reel as it sank down and slowly moved away.

"Yeah, amazing," said Nick, depressed. "What will be even more amazing is what my dad will do to me when he finds out I lost another pole."

Nick seemed to lose at least one pole each summer. It was only June the previous year when his fishing line became tangled in the propeller of the Roberts' outboard engine. When Justin's dad gunned the engine to take off, Nick's pole flew from his hand.

"I remember when you lost your pole last summer,"

Justin recalled. "I've skipped a lot of stones on the lake before, but I never saw anything move across the water faster than that rod and reel."

Somewhere between the camp and the village of Inlet the line snapped and more of Nick's fishing gear headed for the bottom of Fourth Lake.

"Did you hear that?" Justin asked, and stood to his feet.

Nick and Jackie looked at each other, then up at Justin.

"Hear what?" asked Nick.

"I think it's a loon." Justin pointed with one hand and shielded his eyes with the other, squinting into the sun which was moving toward the west end of the lake. The bird was quite a distance away.

Jackie sighed. "It's probably just one of the mallards," she said.

"Yeah," Nick agreed. "You've got loons on the brain today."

Justin ignored them.

"It *is* a loon," he said. "Besides, mallards don't make noises like loons. That was one of those tremble calls, or something like that. Dad said it is the noise loons make when they're in trouble."

Nick used both hands to protect his eyes from the glare of the sun off the water.

"What's that coming in behind it?" asked Nick. "Hey, where did the bird go?"

The bird was indeed gone. It had disappeared and in its place were the silhouettes of two jet skis. Jackie and Nick were scanning the sky to see if the loon had taken flight.

"It dived," said Justin. "It's scared and trying to get away."

Several seconds later the loon resurfaced, but had backtracked under the two water craft and was moving quickly in the opposite direction.

Nick blinked. "Smart bird," he said.

They watched as the jet skis made wide turns and began to bear down on the creature once again.

"Hey!" said Justin loudly. "Those guys are chasing the loon on purpose." He called out louder and started waving his arms. "Stop it!" he yelled. "Stop it!"

"It's no use, Justin," said Jackie. "They're too far away and they couldn't hear you over the sound of those engines anyway."

"I'm getting Dad," Justin cried and ran toward camp.

A few moments later Mr. Robert was peering out over the lake with a pair of binoculars joining the three other sets of eyes on the dock looking for any sign of the bird and renegade jet skiers.

"We couldn't get a good look at them with the sun in our eyes, Mr. Robert," Jackie explained.

"They even tried to get the loon, Dad," said Justin, distressed. "They even tried to run it over. I hate those boats."

"Calm down, Son," urged Mr. Robert. "The boats didn't go after the bird; the people operating the boats caused the mischief. You three sure had fun on Uncle

Bobby's wave runner when he brought it up last summer – didn't you?"

"Well, yes, sort of," admitted Justin.

There was plenty of home video footage in the camp as evidence. He couldn't deny it.

"But we didn't play squish the loonie when we were riding," Nick pointed out in an attempt to come to the aid of his friend. "Justin's Uncle Bobby told us the rules when he took us out, and he said when we were older some day he'd let us drive all by ourselves."

"I liked the kayak better," persisted Justin. "And what if the loon leaves the lake and it has a chick loon – wouldn't the chick loon... die?"

"I know, Justin," said Mr. Robert. "And I agree with you. It's good that you care so much for the birds and their welfare. If we see people out on their water craft riding irresponsibly like that again, we'll try to make some kind of identification and call the sheriff. I promise."

KA-SPLASH!

The sudden eruption of water startled everyone. Nick's t-shirt and sneakers were still on the dock. But Nick wasn't in them.

A few seconds later, his head popped up bobbing in the waves like a buoy. He spit and smiled as he held up his pole.

"It got stuck on a rock and I think there's still a fish on it." Nick grinned. "I really am a loonie!"

No one disagreed.

chapter nine

Shhhhhh!

"Ranger Bill and his wife, Betty, came over to the island last night for dinner," Jackie told the boys at the Rock during an official meeting of Pioneer Village.

Jackie was the only native Adirondack kid among the three friends and lived on the small island until early fall. The rest of the year she lived with her family in a winterized cabin on the mainland.

"Those guys are always at your house," said Nick. "Isn't it weird having the police visit all the time?"

Jackie corrected him. "He's not a policeman," she said. "He is a Forest Ranger. And they've been best friends with my parents for years. What's so weird about that?"

Nick shrugged. "Whatever."

"I asked him about loons on our lake," Jackie continued. "He said there is definitely a nest, but it's kind of a secret where it is."

It had been nearly two weeks since the loon chasing incident. A number of people had now seen the loons and heard them wail and call on the lake. But no one was sure if they were actually raising any chicks there.

"Bucky doesn't want anyone bugging them – that's why he won't say where they are, right?" asked Nick.

"Right," said Jackie. "And please stop calling him Bucky. That's so disrespectful." She gave Nick a stern look. "Anyway, Ranger Bill *Buck* said it's a sign of a really healthy lake if loons are living on it."

"As mayor I vote that Jackie stop treating me like my mother," said Nick.

Justin sighed. "Stop it, Nick," he said, and turned to Jackie. "Did Ranger Rick think the loons will be safe?"

"Well, yes, kind of," said Jackie with some hesitation in her voice. "But he said loon nests are usually really close to the water and big waves can even wash them away."

"There are so many big motorboats around here, especially on the weekends," said Justin. "The waves are always splashing way up on the dock."

"He also talked again about those jet skiers we saw two weeks ago," said Jackie. "If people chase the loons and they have little chicks the baby loons could easily get separated from their parents. Then sea gulls or even big turtles –"

"Would eat them for lunch, right?" finished Nick.

"Yes, that's one way to put it," said Jackie. "And do you know what else? Parent loons only have one or two babies each year – rarely, three."

They all sat quietly for a moment.

"I've got an idea," said Justin, breaking the silence.

"I vote that we make up our own poster about the loons on Fourth Lake and tell people to be extra careful around them."

Jackie agreed. "That's a great idea," she said. "We could even deliver them from dock to dock around the lake using the putt-putt. We could ask Ranger Bill for help and write down all kinds of facts about loons."

"And we could use our computer to make the poster and even find some stuff about loons on the internet," Justin said.

The two were on a roll with their ideas.

"What do you think, Nick?" asked Justin.

"I think all this talk about sea gulls and turtles having lunch has made me hungry," he answered. He stood up and brushed off the seat of his shorts. "I vote we eat."

Nick ran off to his camp for lunch.

Justin and Jackie were too excited about their project to think about food and headed for the Roberts' camp to use the computer. Bounding up the steps and through the screen door, they stood breathless in the den where they discovered Justin's mom was already busy using the machine.

"Mom?" asked Justin. "Can we use the computer?"

"Not right now," she answered. "I'm working on the second draft of this magazine article. It has to be finished and delivered by the end of the week."

"But Mom..." pleaded Justin.

"There's a computer at the public library," Mrs. Robert said with eyes fixed to the computer screen and fingers continuing to dart about the keyboard. "Don't go without eating. There are sandwiches all made in the fridge." She never looked up.

Justin's mom was what the family called, *In A Zone*. She spent hours on the computer writing, shopping and chatting with people all over the world. Justin knew it was useless to beg. He and Jackie skipped the sand- wiches and grabbed a granola bar each as they ran for the boathouse which was connected to the dock.

Inside on the floor were two kayaks, a canoe, a small refrigerator and a container filled with empty soda cans. On the wall hung several colorful life preservers and half a dozen lawn chairs. Bobbing slowly up and down in the water at the center of the building was the Roberts' small motor boat, the *Tamarack*.

Justin's bicycle was also stored inside. So was Jackie's.

"It's great of your parents to let me keep my bike here while we're on the island all summer," Jackie said.

They mounted their two-wheeled transportation and pedaled along the shoulder of Route 28 racing each other toward the local hamlet.

INLET PUBLIC LIBRARY. The brightly painted sign in strong bold letters hung above the front door. Justin and Jackie parked their bikes and entered the simple brick building.

Set back from the highway and sandwiched between the post office and florist shoppe in the center of the hamlet, the library looked small from the outside. But inside hundreds of books in all sizes, shapes and colors were stacked and piled on shelves from the floor to the ceiling in half a dozen rooms. Old black-and-white photographs and a few yellowed maps occupied what little wall space remained. A sofa and two over-sized stuffed chairs under a large plate glass window in the main room provided seating for readers under plenty of natural light.

A small woman with kind eyes, wide smile and gray hair pulled back into a bun greeted them from behind a large hardwood counter as they entered the door.

Neither Jackie nor Justin recognized her.

"May I help you?" she whispered.

Justin and Jackie looked around. There was no one else in the room.

"Why is she whispering?" Justin whispered to Jackie.

"I may be old, but I'm not deaf young man," whispered the woman behind the counter. She never stopped smiling. "We whisper because this...(she stopped and gestured dramatically with one hand sweeping across the entire room)...is a library."

"And this...is really weird," whispered Justin even more softly out of the corner of his mouth toward his friend.

"We'd like to use the computer, please?" whispered Jackie. She forced a smile while gently poking Justin in the ribs.

"Certainly," whispered the woman. She disappeared and suddenly emerged from behind the counter right next to them.

Startled, Justin stood facing her eye to eye. Jackie, a bit taller than both of them, had a clear view right over her head. A small button was pinned to her plain gray dress that read, *Volunteer Librarian*.

She pressed a raised index finger against her slightly parted lips. "Shhhh." Then she motioned for Justin and Jackie to follow her. "Come right this way," she whispered.

Footsteps echoed throughout the large hollow building as they followed the tiny librarian with plain gray shoes across the wooden floor to a small room which like all the others, was lined with shelves of books.

A table with a single computer and printer sat cramped against the wall under a small stained-glass window which provided the room's only light.

"Are you familiar with the operation of a computer?" whispered the librarian.

"Very familiar, thank you," Jackie whispered in reply.

"Hey, is anybody home!" The loud voice of a young boy suddenly bellowed from the lobby.

The librarian gasped. "Oh, my," she said, and quickly shuffled away.

Finally alone, the two researchers relaxed.

"Okay, let's look up the word, *loon*," said Justin.

Jackie sat at the computer and began the search. She typed in, L–O–O–N, and a page showing five different loon species appeared on the screen. "Wow," she said. "There's a Red-Throated Loon, a Black-throated, a Pacific and a Yellow-billed." She clicked on the photo of their loon, the Common Loon. There was a brief description of the bird and an option to hit a key to hear what the loon sounded like. That was all.

"Shhhhhhhh!"

Justin sighed. "There's hardly anything to help us with our poster," he said.

"Try www.loonie.com!" It was Nick. The librarian had discovered the source of all the noise and had directed him to his friends.

"Quiet," whispered Jackie. "The librarian will hear you."

Nick disagreed. "She can't hear us way in here," he said.

A resounding *Shhhhhh* from several rooms away proved him wrong.

Jackie poked a few keys and moaned. "Great, now the library's computer isn't working right," she said. "Now what should we do?"

"Just put a blank page on the screen we can write on," said Justin. "We'll make up a list of rules ourselves."

He tried to remember exactly what the sign had said on the trail head at Moss Lake.

"Start like this," Justin said. "Rule number one – don't chase loons around in your boat."

Nick read aloud as the words Jackie typed appeared on the screen.

"Uh, what would a loon be doing in your boat?" he asked.

"Nick!" groaned Justin.

"I am so sorry, children," came a whisper from behind them. It was the librarian. They were so busy talking they had never even heard her coming. "You are being much, much too loud." She smiled. "Perhaps you can come back another day."

"Kicked out of the library." Jackie shook her head in disbelief as she climbed onto her mountain bike outside. "Thanks a lot, Nick."

"I didn't do anything," insisted Nick. He picked up his bike. "What's taking Justin so long, anyway?"

In a matter of moments their lingering companion emerged from the library clutching a book and a magazine.

"I told the librarian what we were trying to do and she found these for me in just a few seconds." Justin held the two publications face up toward his friends. "Look," he said. "All about loons."

chapter ten

Captain
Conall McBride

Without Nick to distract him, it didn't take Justin long to get his thoughts down on the computer back at camp.

The information about loons contained in the book and magazine provided by the librarian was perfect. One of the articles in the magazine even talked about problems with personal watercraft in the Adirondacks. It seemed Fourth Lake wasn't the only place in the mountains to have some irresponsible boat operators.

He rushed, eager to finish. Except for a picture of the bird, his poster was complete. He plucked the finished sheet out of the printer's tray and hurried from the den to the porch. His mom sat with her eyes closed, her head resting on the wide fan back of her favorite Adirondack chair.

"Wake up, Mom." Justin thrust the paper into her hands. "Can you read this right now – I just need to get a loon picture on it." He expected a rave review.

She smiled and picked up her glass of lemonade. She began to read, then set down her drink and picked up a pen.

Oh no, thought Justin. *Not the pen. There must be a ton of mistakes if she picked up the pen.*

His mom read silently, occasionally making small marks on the copy.

PLEASE LEAVE THE LOONS ALONE!!!

Dear cramp owner, there are loons and babys on our lake. please hang up this poster where everyone cans see it please!

Rule #1 Please do not dive your oats
fast and make pig waves. it might ruin the
nests
Rule #2 Please donut chase loons so they get
scared and fly away and dont ever come
back
Rule #3 Please dont chase loons so their
baby chick loons get beaten by turtles
Rule #4 Please do not get to close to
loons ever
Rule #5 Please do not chase goons on
jet skis
If you see someone chasing lions you can call
Ranger Bill Duck his number is 31%-962-1009

P.S. Good loon books are at the Inlet Libary

"Well, there are some very good rules here, Justin," said his mother. "And you have been very polite."

Justin beamed.

"Did you happen to proof read this at all yourself?" she asked.

Justin hung his head slowly. "Well, no, not really," he said.

"Did you use the computer's spell check?" she asked.

"Uh... no," he said.

Mrs. Robert made a few more scribbles on the sheet and handed it back to him.

"Other than those few spelling and grammatical corrections I would not change a thing," she told him. "Fix them and then I'll scan one of your father's loon pictures you can use as an illustration."

"Thanks, Mom!" Justin started to rush back into the camp when a strange horn sounded from the lake. Both he and his mother moved toward the edge of the porch and peered down toward the dock.

Justin looked puzzled. "What kind of a boat is that?"

He ran down to the dock for a closer look. Mrs. Robert followed.

The long wooden vessel was open at the bow which was lined with several rows of seats. Toward the stern stood a large cabin with several large open windows. A bright blue canopy draped over the seats billowed in the breeze. To Justin it looked like a small house on a boat.

Yes, it's a house boat, he thought. The mystery craft slowed down and inched its way alongside the dock, engine thundering.

"The name's McBride," called the man at the helm.

"Captain Conall McBride."

He tipped his weathered baseball cap as part of his introduction. Then he sneezed.

"I'll be delivering mail along the chain of lakes," the captain called. He leaned with one hand out over the water and handed an envelope to Mrs. Robert. He tipped his hat again, sneezed again, and motored away toward the dock next door.

"What is it, Mom?" asked Justin.

"It looks like a letter," Mrs. Robert answered. She ripped open the envelope and pulled out a small note that was tucked inside and read it out loud.

Dear Lake Resident,

Five years ago, I retired from the navy and bought the old mail boat, "Miss America." She was in rough shape and all this time I have worked to restore her to her former glory.

She's ready to sail now and two days a week all summer I'll be delivering letters and packages around Fourth Lake.

There's no charge for deliveries, but anyone can ride the historic boat for five dollars.

Watch for me on Wednesdays and Saturdays. When you hear the horn, come running to pick up and drop off your mail.

Be sure to hurry, "Miss America" stays on the move.

Sincerely,
Captain Conall McBride

"I read something about this in the *Express* last week," Mrs. Robert recalled.

The *Adirondack Express* was the Central Adirondack's local newspaper and carried all the interesting news, notes, and photographs of the region.

"I remember now," she said. "The captain has a camp somewhere over on the south shore."

"Uh huh," said Justin. His thoughts were drifting. It had suddenly occurred to him how he and Jackie and Nick could deliver the posters to help their loons.

chapter eleven

The Arcade

Rain. It seemed to control the behavior of everyone in the mountains. Especially the tourists and campers who headed for the stores and restaurants of the small resort hamlets and villages under stormy skies.

Justin, Jackie and Nick were not exceptions. The three Adirondack kids headed for the Arcade in Old Forge which was always packed inside when it was pouring outside.

SWISH. ZHEEER. KA-BOOM!

"I love this game," said Nick. He was busy pushing buttons at an impressive rate on his favorite machine and destroying the alien space ships racing across the screen. A crowd began to gather around him to watch.

Justin and Jackie were standing in the open doorway of the building, away from all the activity. They were trapped between the flashing lights, bells and whistles and the pounding summer downpour.

Jackie reached outside and let the cool rain water wash over her hand.

"I don't know what Nick will do if they ever get rid of that game," she said. "Every year he shows off for the new kids on it."

"The owners will never get rid of it," said Justin. He watched the rain drops collect and stream through Jackie's finger into an expanding puddle on the ground. "Not with all the quarters he's put into it. Actually, they should just give the game to him."

"Comin' through!" Four older boys pushed their way past Justin and Jackie through the open archway and disappeared into the arcade. Each boy seemed to hit the puddle dead center as they ran by, splashing muddy water in all directions.

"Nice, real nice," said Jackie as she looked down on her white sneakers, socks and shorts, now speckled brown. "And I'm sure that was by accident."

"Since when has a little dirt bothered you?" asked Justin. "Let's go back in and get something to eat."

Nick had just finished his public performance on *Invasion of the Space Aliens!* and joined them at the snack bar.

"I am the master," boasted Nick. "Even though it was only my second highest score ever."

"You're slipping," Justin chided. "The planet earth is depending on you."

They sat at one of the indoor picnic tables, sipping on sodas and munching fries.

"I've got to go to the bathroom," Nick said. "Don't you dare touch my fries."

He plucked several of them out of the package, licked them and put them back.

"Now they'll be safe," he said.

"Grrrrosss," said Jackie. She watched Nick run off

and frowned after him in disgust. Then she smiled.

"I've got an idea," she said, and ran over to a cluster of small vending machines that stood together against the wall near the entrance of the building.

Justin watched as Jackie examined the contents through the clear bubble tops of each container. Two were filled with colored neon bouncy balls. One was filled with key chains and another with candy. She quickly shoved two quarters into the coin slot of a machine teeming with weird little rubber bugs. Dozens of small gushy red, yellow and green insect bodies with their teeny antennae and legs pressed up against the glass.

"There," Jackie said, as she rushed back to the picnic table and slipped a small green bug in among Nick's french fries.

Justin laughed and choked on his soda. "Hurry, sit down," he told Jackie, and quickly wiped his mouth with the back of his hand. "Here he comes."

Nick was running toward them. He looked panic-stricken. Justin and Jackie were too busy with their plan to notice.

"Do you think he saw me?" asked Jackie.

Justin looked down and took another sip of soda. "Just act normal," he said.

"Hey, you guys," Nick said, leaning against the table to catch his breath.

"Finish your fries," urged Justin.

Jackie chimed in. "Yes, hurry up and eat. They're getting cold."

Nick ignored them. "No, listen," he said, still panting. "I heard those guys who splashed Jackie talking in the bathroom. I think two of them are those jet ski guys – you know – the ones playing squish the loonie."

"How do you know it was them?" asked Jackie.

Justin's face was bright red. "What did they say!"

Nick took a deep breath. "Well, they were laughing and bragging and stuff about how fast they could go on their boats," he said. "And one of them said, 'you should see those stupid ducks move when they have to.'"

Justin stood up. "Come on, let's find them," he said. "Dad said if we could describe who was hurting the loons, he would call the sheriff. He promised."

"Then we better go right now," said Nick. "They are running out the door."

Justin and Jackie turned to see the backs of four bodies dashing out into the heavy rain and took off after them. Nick grabbed his fries and ran close behind.

It was still pouring hard. The rain stung as it hit their faces and it was difficult to run with their heads up.

Justin was in the lead, chasing blindly after the boys who were quickly pulling away. Racing on, he wiped his eyes with the palms of his hands.

WHAP!

Justin ran smack into a pedestrian on the street. He looked up squinting into the rain.

A large frame of a man without a face loomed over him. Justin shivered.

"Whoa, what's your hurry there, young fellow?"

A large frame of a man without a face
towered over him. Justin shivered.

The booming, but jolly voice came from somewhere within the hood of the giant's dark blue rain slicker.

Justin thought he sounded familiar.

Jackie and Nick quickly caught up and joined Justin in front of the towering man.

"Why don't we step out of the rain," the friendly giant suggested, and they all took cover under the marquee of the local movie theater.

Justin quickly introduced himself and his two friends. "I'm sorry I ran into you like that," he said.

The man pulled back the hood of his slicker.

"You're the mail boat captain!" Justin said.

The man laughed out loud. "That's right, I am," he said. "Captain Conall McBride soon serving the Fulton Chain and beginning next Wednesday with Fourth Lake."

"I really wanted to meet you," Justin said. "You handed my mom a letter at our dock the other day."

"I remember the stop," said the captain.

"Well, Jackie and Nick and I were kind of hoping we could deliver some posters to all the camps on the lake, telling people to watch out for our loons. We were going to use Jackie's motor boat, but you have a loud horn and people know you're coming and –"

The captain interrupted. "And I think you three have a very worthy cause there," he said. "It would be my honor to help you deliver your posters around the lake. A noble cause worthy of *Miss America's* maiden voyage."

"Really?" Justin said. "That's great."

"Yes," said the captain. "My assistant Dax and I will meet you at eight o'clock sharp at your dock on Wednesday morning. You will need about fifty copies of your poster for our first tour."

"Ahhhh!" screamed Nick.

Everyone turned. The cry was so startling even an usher from inside the movie theater rushed out to see what had happened.

Nick's soggy french fries were strewn all over the sidewalk and down onto the steps. In the midst of them lay a small green bug.

chapter twelve

A Close Call

"Meet my assistant, Dax," said Captain McBride talking loudly over the noise of the mail boat engine. Then he sneezed.

It was Wednesday morning. The sun was already hot. The deep blue lake encircled by low mountains all around matched the color of the cloudless sky.

Justin, Jackie and Nick had boarded *Miss America* and were already headed for the first dock on the waterway mail route, loon posters in hand.

"Where is he?" asked Justin. "Your assistant?"

"Not he, *she*," answered the captain.

Justin quickly scanned the wide, open bow of the boat which was equipped with its four rows of wooden passenger seats. All empty.

Nick emerged from the small cabin which housed both the mail, and the captain at the wheel. "There's nobody in there but the captain," he called.

A large, sleek calico cat suddenly appeared on the cabin roof, looking down at the top of Nick's head.

"I think I found her," said Jackie and smiled.

"Where?" asked Nick. He looked quickly left, right and behind.

"Nice to meet you, Dax." Jackie pointed to the spot just above Nick's head. He slowly turned and looked up.

"Dax is a *cat*?" Nick was surprised.

They all were.

Ah-choo! The captain sneezed again.

"She came with the boat when I bought her," said the captain. He wiped his nose. "The problem is I'm allergic to cats. But Dax knows every nook and cranny of this old vessel. She even slept nights in the boat while I was fixing it up. She knows *Miss America* better than I do."

The captain sounded the horn and slowed the boat as they approached dock number one.

"We don't come to a full stop," he said. "We move along very slowly dockside and exchange any letters and packages."

"Yoo-hoo. Yoo-hoo. Don't leave. Don't leave."

An elderly lady calling out in a high-pitched voice was moving as fast as she could from her lakeside camp down a set of stairs leading to the dock.

"However, today we will make an exception," the captain said.

"She's waving something in her hand," said Justin. "I think it's a postcard."

"Oh, my," said the lady as she approached the boat.

She was puffing and catching her breath. It was hard to hear over the idling engine of the boat.

"I didn't think I'd make it," she said. "But I did so want to send this little card to my friend across the lake."

She handed the postcard to the captain who stood leaning out the cabin window. Justin offered the lady a poster as the boat began to pull away from the dock.

"Please read this," Justin said. The engine grew louder and the boat began to move.

"There are loons on our lake," he shouted to the woman who appeared smaller and smaller as they pushed on. Justin cupped his hands around his mouth and yelled even louder. "We need to protect them!"

The woman was already a speck on the shoreline.

"We'll have to make better time at each dock if we're going to reach everybody at this end of the lake before noon," the captain said.

Most of the docks were empty, but posters were successfully delivered to some kids fishing, an artist working on a painting of the mountains and one man flying a remote-controlled seaplane.

While a few people had simple notes and cards ready to send to their neighbors, many more were simply curious and stood on their docks just to wave.

Everyone was surprised to receive a piece of mail the very first day – Justin's loon poster.

"We still have some posters left," said Justin as the mail boat completed its run along the perimeter of the lake's eastern end.

"I'm bored," said Nick. He was sitting in the second row of chairs playing a hand-held video game. "I sure couldn't do this delivery stuff two days a week. There's nothing exciting. There's nothing to do. Just stop and go and stop and go and –"

"Stop," said Jackie. She sat relaxed in the row just in front of him. Dax was resting on her lap. "You don't have to spoil the ride for the rest of us."

"We'll just make a turn around Cedar Island," said the captain. "We don't want to leave anyone out."

As the captain prepared to maneuver the boat around the island, they all heard a low buzzing noise.

"What's that?" asked Jackie.

"It sounds like that guy's remote-controlled plane," Nick said.

"No, not that." Jackie stood up and Dax jumped down from her lap and bounded up onto the railing. "*That*."

She pointed to two duck-shaped silhouettes moving just ahead in unison across the water.

"They're the loons," Justin said, excitedly. "I'll bet it's the mom and the dad."

The birds moved around the end of the island and out of sight. The boat moved in a similar direction, but made a much wider arc out into deeper water before attempting the turn. Without the island as a buffer, the buzzing noise grew violently louder, almost deafening.

Nick was right. It was a plane. But not a two-foot remote-controlled seaplane. It was the real thing. And it was just lifting off the lake, but in a direct path with the slow and awkward moving mail boat.

Justin saw the loons, now fully back in view, open their beaks and dive.

That seemed like a great idea.

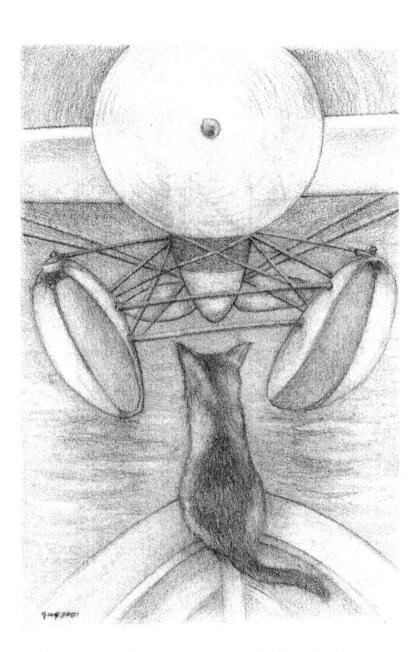

"Dax sat confidently and watched as the bottom
of the plane's pontoons soared above the boat."

All three of the Adirondack kids hit the deck. Justin dropped into the open bow. Jackie and Nick fell between the empty rows of chairs. Dax was oblivious. She just sat propped confidently on the rail and watched as the bottom of the plane's pontoons soared no more than two feet over the top of the boat. Her fur moved with the breeze created by the aircraft.

The captain remained at the wheel, his face as white as his beard.

As the buzz of the plane became more faint, Jackie turned her head and made eye contact with Nick between the chair legs.

Lying there face to face she grinned at him.

"Still bored?" she asked.

chapter thirteen

Dax Attacks

Justin felt good as he sat on the stairs at camp in the early morning sun waiting for Nick to stop by. They were going fishing.

His parents were in the kitchen eating breakfast and he was using the quiet time to reflect on the events of one day earlier with great satisfaction. Thirty-four loon posters delivered. And Captain McBride had promised to deliver as many more as he could.

More people watching out for our loons, Justin thought.

Meow.

Justin bent over and looked between his legs under the stairs.

Meow.

"Dax!" Justin said. "How did you get here?"

The calico cat slipped up between the wood steps and began to move in a slow figure eight rubbing against Justin's legs, purring softly.

Justin reached down to pet her. She was soft, but firm. No fat. All muscle. Not at all like his chubby, fluffy house cat, Socks, back at home with Grandpa. She was all patches and streaks of black and white and rufous. Her most distinguished mark? A large black triangle ran from the middle of her forehead sweeping down at an angle underneath her right eye to her cheek, strait across to her nose, and back up to her forehead.

"What are you doing here?" he asked out loud again as he stroked the length of her body. "What's the captain going to do without you today?"

"Probably enjoy a whole day without sneezing." It was Nick with a pole and worm in hand. "Let's get going. My worm is getting kind of mushy."

Together the two headed toward the dock. Dax tagged along, remaining close to Justin.

All the early morning fog had burned off the lake. There was no wind. The surrounding mountains reflected perfectly onto the water's glassy surface.

As Justin and Nick sat with their legs crossed at the edge of the dock and cast their lines, Dax headed for the nearest boat – the two-seat kayak – the one Justin and his dad had used at Moss Lake. She jumped aboard and disappeared under the bow.

"Exploring," Justin said. He could hear scratching sounds and watched over his shoulder as the kayak vibrated slightly from the inquisitive cat's presence inside. "You should feel how strong she is. I'll bet it's from living up here in the wilderness – all the exercise and everything."

"That cat sure loves boats," Nick said. "Remember the captain said she just about lived in *Miss America*, and there she is running now all over the inside of your boat."

The quiet out on the lake was broken by the hum of a small engine. No – two small engines.

Nick glanced off to his right and down along the shoreline of the lake. He moaned. "Oh no, not again!"

A pair of mallard ducks were flushed from their early morning swim. Their stout wings beat quickly and carried them up and out of harm's way.

Sunlight flashed off the bodies of two jet skis engaged in the chase.

"That's it," Justin said. "I'm not waiting anymore." He dropped his pole and headed for camp. Within seconds he was back carrying his dad's camera.

"Let's go," he said.

"Go where?" asked Nick.

Justin handed Nick the camera and ran into the boathouse. He came out wearing a life jacket and handed one to Nick.

"Come on. You're getting in front and I'll paddle. If we can get close enough, you can take a picture of those guys and Ranger Bill can identify them."

Nick hesitated. "I don't know, Justin." He looked out toward the fast moving water craft which were still speeding and twisting about at the command of the drivers. There was a hint of fear in his eyes. He slowly donned his life jacket.

"Come on, help me, hurry," urged Justin. He was trying to manipulate the kayak off the dock and into the lake.

Nick looped the camera strap around his neck and took hold of his end of the boat. Together the two friends eased it into the water. Nick climbed into the front seat. The boat rocked. Justin grabbed the paddle, settled into the rear and they shoved off.

Meow.

"Dax!" said Nick as the calico cat popped up between his two legs and looked at him.

"Get ready," Justin called out. "Get ready to take a picture." He paddled furiously but was only inching the kayak toward the action.

Nick grabbed the camera that dangled loosely around his neck at the end of the long strap and looked at the front of the camera lens. *Click-Click-Click.*

"Oops," said Nick.

"Be careful," Justin said. "There's a motor thing dad uses on that camera. It can take a whole bunch of pictures in just a few seconds."

The jet skis continued to make small circles, change direction quickly and dodge one another. Then they made one more turn and together began to speed directly toward the kayak.

Something was in the water between the motor boats and the paddlers.

"There's a loon!" cried Justin, and paddled harder. His technique was miserable. He applied nothing about paddling he had learned from his father at Moss Lake. The paddle splashed into the water on one side, and then on the other. Sometimes the paddle banged against the side of the boat and he missed a stroke altogether. Still, the kayak jerked forward.

"Get ready, Nick. Get ready," he said.

Nick was trembling. He fumbled with the camera and lifted the view finder to his eye. The scenes he saw through the lens moved up and down and all around. First he saw the sky. Then the water. Then the shoreline. Then...*Dax*?

The cat had climbed out of the cockpit and now stood balanced out on the kayak's narrow bow.

Nick turned and called back to Justin over his shoulder. "Can't you keep us steady? I'm getting dizzy looking through the camera." He turned back toward the bow. "Get back in here, Dax!" he said.

The jet skis moved in on the loon.

The loon dived.

One of the jet skis slowed down, made a wide turn and began to circle back.

"I think they figured out the loonie's trick," said Nick. He was now beginning to shake.

The second jet ski continued to move directly at the kayak. A steady stream of water streaked high into the air at the rear of the craft. Details became clearer in the machine moving toward them now. Both Nick and Justin could finally make out the boat's brilliant ebony body.

Then closer.

They could see the body trimmed with yellow stripes. It looked like a huge hornet skimming across the water straight at them.

Then closer.

They could see the driver's hair, eyes, nose and mischievous grin.

"Take a picture," yelled Justin. "Take one now."

Nick raised the camera and pointed it in the direction of the jet ski. Justin stopped paddling.

The driver stopped grinning. In fact, his grin turned into a frown as he recognized it was a camera in Nick's hands. He sped by inches from the side of the kayak.

Nick closed his eyes and pressed the button to take a picture as the jet ski went by. *Click-click-click-click.*

A spray of water washed into the kayak and all across the paddlers, the camera and Dax.

Justin and Nick were in shock. And confused. They hadn't expected such a direct attack by the young boater. The kayak rocked in the wave.

"Oh, no, here he comes again," cried Nick. He dropped the camera which fell over the side of the kayak into the lake. It still dangled at the end of the long strap around his neck and slapped against the side of the boat, fully submerged in the water. He ducked down as far as he could to help stabilize the vessel. Justin did, too.

As the jet ski made its second aggressive pass by the paralyzed vessel, Dax leapt from the kayak and onto the back of the driver, who let out an abrupt scream. The jet ski sped away and began weaving with Dax clinging to the neck and life jacket of the operator.

Justin and Nick slowly sat up and opened their eyes in disbelief. The assault was over and the jet skiers were gone.

So was the loon.

And so was Dax.

"Take a picture," said Justin. *"Take one now!"*

Suddenly the sound of another engine approached them from behind.

"Oh, no," they cried in unison, and ducked down again.

This time it was a motorboat. Moving wide of their position on the lake it was pulling an elderly female water-skier sporting a one-piece bathing suit decorated with more bright colors than a rainbow. With one hand grasping the tow rope, she turned slightly and with the other waved to the boys.

Another chase was on. This time it was the jet skiers who were running.

chapter fourteen

Grounded

Justin paddled slowly back to the Roberts' dock. Still shaken, the two boys' spirits were as damp as the camera, their clothes and their pride.

No pictures. No Dax. And no good explanation to their parents for their irresponsible behavior.

The kayak finally came to rest against the dock. The boys meekly raised their heads to face the adults already waiting there to greet them.

"How could you just take off like that?" Justin's mother made direct and unwavering eye contact with him. "What were you thinking?"

He could tell she wasn't really angry. It was worse than that. She was disappointed. He had hurt his mom bad, really bad.

Mr. Robert was standing right next to her.

"Come on boys, out of the boat," he said, and held the kayak steady as the two climbed up onto the dock. It was then he noticed the water dripping from the camera.

"Uh, we sort of had an accident," said Nick. He handed the camera to Mr. Robert. "We had some pictures on it, but they all got ruined."

"Get me the bait pail out of the boathouse, Justin," said Mr. Robert. "Nick, you had better head for home now. We will talk with your parents later."

For once Nick didn't offer back a wise remark. He bolted for the pathway home.

Justin quickly returned with the bait pail. His father took the five-gallon container to the edge of the lake, filled it with water and plunged the camera into it where it settled to the bottom.

"What are you doing, Dad?" Justin watched in disbelief.

"Go to your room now, Son," Mr. Robert replied. "We'll talk later."

Justin laid on his bed tossing and turning. It was still early in the day, not even noon. Light poured in on him. It felt all wrong.

You only go to bed during the daytime when you're sick, he thought.

He felt awful. His parents were upset because he left without telling them, unsupervised, in a boat. They didn't even know yet about the water battle. And what about Dax?

He glanced down at the comic book laying on the floor. The one he had found in the box in the ground. The wild-eyed pilot flying out of control on the cover only underscored his helpless situation.

Stupid comic, Justin thought. *Stupid comic, stupid jet skis, stupid... me.*

He could hear the muffled sound of his parents' voices coming from downstairs.

What are they saying? What are they thinking? Justin tossed some more.

He heard the front screen door squeak open and bang close. Then there were three muffled voices. The door opened and closed again. Back to two voices.

Then it happened again. The front door opened and banged closed. And again, three voices. It was definitely a woman's voice. And she was really loud.

What is going on down there? His thirty minutes of exile so far felt more like thirty hours.

"Justin, would you come down here please?" Mrs. Robert called.

What fate awaited him down the stairs? Would he be grounded for the rest of the summer? Would he be grounded for the rest of his life? Would he ever be allowed to see Nick again?

He took his time. His legs felt heavy, and each limp foot dropped on a descending step with a hollow slap.

He was about two-thirds of the way down the stairs where he squatted to peer through the rails and out onto the floor toward the living room.

First he saw his parents' feet. Then he saw a pair of bare feet. Then he saw what looked like a small puddle of water, and four cat's feet.

"Dax!"

Justin skipped steps the rest of the way down the stairs and burst into the room.

Without looking up, he knelt down and ran his hands like a squeegee along the cat's body pressing hard against her short, wet fur. More water oozed onto the floor. Dax purred.

"I have never seen anything like it," the loud woman said. "And then somehow that boy on that fast little boat unfastened his life preserver and it dropped with the poor kitty into the lake."

Justin stood up and faced the woman who was about his height. It was the lady with the bright bathing suit who had passed him and Nick in pursuit of the renegade water craft. And then he recognized her.

chapter fifteen

A Grand Finale

"It was the *librarian*?" Nick said. "No way."

"Yes, way," said Justin.

Dax had been returned to the captain, and it was the first meeting on *The Rock* at Pioneer Village in a week. It was the first day of freedom for Justin and Nick after seven days of tightly controlled activity by their parents apart from one another.

"Gee, I guess you really can't tell a book by its cover, can you?" Nick laughed out loud at his own pun.

Justin and Jackie looked at each other and rolled their eyes.

"Anyway," Justin continued, "she couldn't keep chasing the guys on the jet skis so she could save Dax. And then she saw our kayak on the dock and stopped and told my parents everything. She said she knew about the loons, too, because the captain took a poster to the library."

"I guess a lot of people saw what happened," Jackie said. "And those posters are everywhere now. My parents even heard people talking about it down at Kalil's grocery store."

"A lot of good it's all done," Justin said, flatly. "I'm the one in trouble. Not those bad kids chasing the loons. Mom and Dad said I'm not old enough to be trusted with my own kayak yet. And somehow I've got to pay Dad back for his ruined camera."

"How much will that cost?" asked Jackie.

"Dad said it's something like six hundred dollars," Justin said. "It's old, but it's really valuable."

"Six hundred dollars!" Jackie said.

"Maybe you could collect cans on Route 28 and at the campsites and stuff," Nick said.

"I can help," Jackie offered.

"I vote we go use Justin's computer calculator to see how many cans we need," Nick said.

Everyone agreed. The three Adirondack kids ended the meeting and headed for Justin's camp.

"Hey, I wonder what Ranger Bill is doing here?" asked Jackie. She noticed his motorboat tied to the Roberts' dock.

"Mom, can I use the computer?" Justin called out as he and his friends entered the front door.

"Justin, come here a minute." It was his dad.

Ranger Bill and Mr. and Mrs. Robert were seated around the kitchen table. Several photographs lay in the center of the table between them.

"I didn't want to get your hopes up, Son, but it seems one of the photographs Nick took during your little adventure last week was clear enough for the sheriff to make a positive identification."

"What?" Justin was stunned.

Nick began to strut about the kitchen waving his arms in the air and looking for high-fives. "I'm the man, yes, I'm the man."

There on the table was the entire series of photographs Nick had taken. Several were of Nick's own face including close-ups of his nose. Three were blurry images showing part shoreline, part sky. One was of Dax in mid-air. And one, just one, showed a full frontal close-up view of the water craft and its rider as it pressed in on the side of the kayak.

"Hey, that's the one I took with my eyes closed," said Nick.

"It's one of the guys from the arcade!" said Justin.

Jackie blushed. "That stain from the mud puddle still hasn't come out of my shorts or my t-shirt," she said.

"The authorities have already visited his home and the home of his friend," Ranger Bill said. "This is their first summer in the Adirondacks and they are learning there is a right way and a wrong way to have fun here."

"What's going to happen to them?" Justin asked. He actually felt kind of sorry they were in such big trouble.

"We are arranging to have them do some volunteer community service," Ranger Bill said. "One of their jobs will be to learn about loons and help distribute your poster, Justin. And they will not be riding any water craft on Adirondack lakes again this summer."

Justin looked puzzled.

"But Dad, I thought the camera was ruined. You even threw it into the bait pail. I don't get it."

"Well, the camera is ruined," said Mr. Robert. "But by keeping the film inside the camera soaked, we were still able to salvage it at the processing plant. There were a few pictures on the roll I had taken earlier I was also hoping to save."

"Your father drove all the way to Utica to have the film processed," said Mrs. Robert.

Justin hung his head.

"I really am sorry about your camera, Dad," he said.

"Me, too," said Nick.

"Mom, if you're not using the computer, can we use it now?" Justin asked.

"Sure honey, what for?" she asked.

"We want to figure out how many cans Justin has to collect to earn six hundred dollars," said Nick.

"12,000," said Mr. Robert.

"12,000 what?" asked Justin.

"Cans," he answered. "At a nickel each, you'll need 12,000 cans to raise six hundred dollars."

Justin frowned and his shoulders slumped.

Nick shook his head in amazement. "You can figure that out in your head?"

Mrs. Robert glanced over at Mr. Robert. He nodded.

"Justin, you know the comic book you found that you are not that fond of?" Mrs. Robert asked.

"Yes," Justin said.

"Well, I found someone on the internet who is willing to buy it from you, if you really don't want it," she said.

"How much?" Justin asked. He really did like comic

books and thought maybe he would keep it.

"Apparently it's the only copy of *Adirondack Sky Pilot* known to exist," she explained. "How does a thousand dollars sound?"

"One - thousand - dollars!" exclaimed Justin in disbelief.

"Hey, I'll trade you the wooden soldier for it," Nick said. "I'll even throw in that old fishing lure."

"I wouldn't be too quick to give away those fishing lures either," Mrs. Robert said. "According to my research, they are quite valuable as well."

"As is that nickel, Jackie," said Mr. Robert.

"It really was buried treasure," said Nick. "We're rich!"

"My mom, the computer whiz," said Justin. He really wanted to hug her, but not in front of his friends.

"After paying for your father's camera, that will leave you with four hundred dollars toward your own kayak," said Mrs. Robert.

Justin's eyes lit up.

"Toward your own kayak for next year," she added quickly.

Justin's eyes lowered. "Yes, Mom," he said, softly.

Mr. Robert chimed in. "Both you and Nick behaved just as irresponsibly as those boys on the jet skis," he said.

"That's right," said Mrs. Robert. "You know, when your father was your age, he –"

"That's all right, honey, I think they get the point," interrupted Mr. Robert.

"Dad did what, Mom?" asked Justin. "What did he do?"

Just then the mail boat horn sounded. The blast was loud and long.

"Saved by the bell," said Mrs. Robert quietly to her husband.

"I wonder why he's stopping," said Justin. "He's only supposed to stop when there's someone on the dock."

Justin, Jackie and Nick along with Ranger Bill and Mr. and Mrs. Robert headed down to the lake to greet the captain.

"Hello there folks!" Captain McBride waved from the wheel. The mail boat idled a few feet from the end of the dock. "It seems for some reason Dax here is very fond of Justin," he said. "Every time I approach your place, she starts pacing and gets all ready to jump."

Even as he spoke Dax stood on the cabin roof looking repeatedly down at the water, then up at the dock. She appeared ready to spring.

"And I must admit," the captain continued, "I have grown quite weary of sneezing all day long."

He gunned the engine just enough to keep the boat from drifting too close to the dock, then idled again.

"Mr. and Mrs. Robert," he called out, "if it's not imposing too much, do you think Dax might join your family?"

"Mom? Dad?" asked Justin, hopefully.

They nodded.

Captain McBride let the boat drift a little closer to the dock. Dax leaped from her perch on top of the mail boat and landed at Justin's feet. She made the jump with plenty of room to spare.

The captain smiled, tipped his hat and maneuvered the mail boat away.

Everyone waved except Justin. His arms were full, with Dax.

Everyone waved except Justin.
His arms were full, with Dax.

epilogue

The evening air was crisp and cool. A slight breeze passed through the screens and across the length of the sleeping porch. Justin pulled the covers up to his neck and adjusted his head on his puffy pillow. It would be a good sleeping night.

Dax was in the boathouse. The wild-eyed pilot wasn't staring at him from the floor any more. He'd soon be rich. And his loons were safe.

He yawned and closed his eyes.

It's funny how things can look so awful one minute and then so great the next, he thought.

The wail of a loon echoed out across the lake.

Justin still considered it an eerie sound, but natural now, even peaceful.

And the summer's just begun, he thought. And then he was asleep.

🐾🔷 DAX FACTS

The **Common Loon** is a migrating bird species arriving on Adirondack lakes following the ice melt in the spring, leaving for wintering grounds in late autumn before the ice returns. They are similar in size to a goose, with feathers during the breeding season that are black-and-white, and they have red eyes.

Common Loons spend almost their entire lives in the water. They can hold their breath for up to five minutes and reach underwater depths of more than 200 feet. This is because their bodies are designed primarily for diving and swimming underwater to catch food and to avoid danger.

Adult Common Loons have red eyes and a dagger-like bill. The breeding plumage includes a black head, white-striped necklace and a back checkered with black and white feathers.
Photo © 2020 Gary VanRiper

Floating nest rafts are sometimes used to help Common Loons successfully hatch and raise their young when on a lake where water levels are known to flood the shoreline.
Photo © 2020 Gary VanRiper

Nests, with one or two eggs (rarely three), are located at the water's edge allowing the birds to slip quickly and quietly in and out of the water. Man-made nesting rafts are sometimes placed on lakes where there is often flooding that causes nests to fail.

The haunting calls of loons at night can be comfort to those familiar with the sounds, but can bring chills to those who hear them for the first time.

There are many threats to the health and welfare of loons including lead poisoning from accidentally eating lost sinkers and other lead fishing tackle. Another threat is humans getting too close to nesting sites when the birds are raising their young. Binoculars and telephoto lenses are helpful tools to observe and enjoy loons from a safe distance.

An adult Common Loon passing a fish to a juvenile. These birds will also eat salamanders, crayfish, leeches, snails and frogs. They will also swallow small stones to crush their food aiding digestion! Photo © 2020 Gary VanRiper

Because the Common Loon is such a strong symbol and voice of the northern wilderness, this amazing bird is mentioned in several volumes of *The Adirondack Kids*® book series, including in volumes 1, 13, 15 & 20.

Learn more about Common Loons from *The Adirondack Center for Loon Conservation*. As of this writing the center is located in Saranac Lake, New York. (www.adkloon.org)

Among vocalizations of the Common Loon are the hoot, wail, yodel, and tremolo. Justin was 12-years-old and using a 200mm lens from his kayak when taking this shot of a vocalizing loon. Photo © 2020 Justin VanRiper

HELP PROTECT LOONS

LOONS, THEIR CHICKS AND NEST SITES
ARE PROTECTED BY
NEW YORK STATE AND FEDERAL LAW

- Disturbance of loons during the nesting season may lead to nest abandonment.

- When boating, steer clear of loons, especially family groups with chicks.

- Do not drive loons away from sheltered areas into open water where boat traffic is heavy.

- Please enjoy and respect this symbol of wilderness by staying as far away from them as possible.

N.Y.S. DEPARTMENT OF ENVIRONMENTAL CONSERVATION

Photo © 2020 Gary VanRiper

 # DAX FACTS

The **35mm Film Camera**. The technology used to take photographs has changed over the years. Today, many people simply use their phones!

The older 35mm camera Justin and Nick used in the story captures photographs on rolls of film. And here is how it works:

First, you pop open the back of the camera using the rewind knob and seat the canister of film into the pocket on the left-hand side.

Then you pull the film leader across to secure the roll in the take-up spool on the right-hand side.

Next, close the camera's back and snap a few shots to advance the film.

35mm Film Camera

Film Canister

35mm cameras have been made by companies like Minolta, Kodak, Nikon, and Canon. Photographer Oskar Barnak invented what became the first commercially successful 35mm camera, the Leica, in 1913 at Ernst Leitz Optische Werke (company) in Wetzlar, Germany.

Photo © 2020 Gary VanRiper

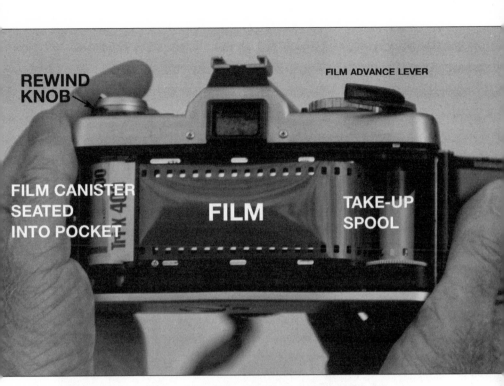

REWIND KNOB

FILM ADVANCE LEVER

FILM CANISTER SEATED INTO POCKET

FILM

TAKE-UP SPOOL

The "leader" is film that is pulled out of the canister to attach to the spool. Only the film that remains in total darkness inside the canister can be used to take photographs.
Photo © 2020 Carol VanRiper

When the number '1' appears in a small window on top of the camera, you are ready to start taking pictures. (Most rolls of film only take 12, 24 or 36 pictures!)

When the last shot on the roll of film is taken, use the rewind knob to roll the film back into the canister. Finally, reopen the camera's back – remove the canister and send it to a processing plant where chemicals are used to develop the film.

Photographs are printed on special paper from the film's processed negatives.

(That was why in the story Mr. Robert put the camera into the bucket of water! He knew the camera was ruined, but needed to keep the film wet. If the film inside the camera had dried out before being processed, all the pictures he and the boys had taken would have been ruined as well!).

89

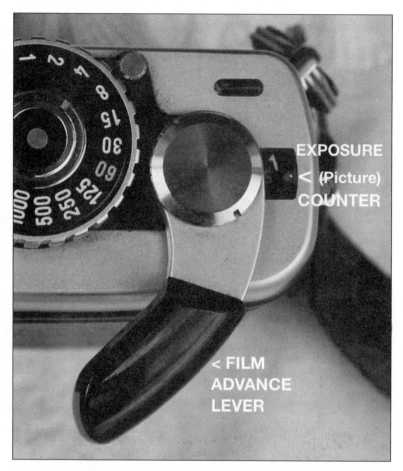

EXPOSURE
< (Picture)
COUNTER

< FILM
ADVANCE
LEVER

Once the film is loaded and the back of the camera closed to seal out all light, photographers use their thumbs to rotate the film advance lever to pull the film from inside the canister into position to take a picture when the shutter button is pushed or "snapped."
Photo © 2020 Gary VanRiper

Sometimes you would have to wait several days or weeks to see how your photographs came out!

Some photographers still use film cameras, but most cameras today are digital and use memory cards, instead of film, to record images. Some camera memory cards can hold hundreds of photographs, and the results can be viewed right away.

As technology continues to change, the way we take photographs will continue to change as well!

 DAX FACTS

Mail boat delivery began on the Fulton Chain of Lakes in the west-central Adirondacks at the turn of the 20th century. Local historians have suggested the 23rd President of the United States, Benjamin Harrison, who had a camp on Second Lake, was instrumental in securing the mail service there.

Official approval for mail delivery along the chain's waterway from Old Forge to Inlet was granted to the Fulton Navigation Company in 1901. The first boat used was called the *Zip*, but was renamed, *Old Forge*.*

Leon Burnap secured the contract for service in 1929 and his brother, Donald, delivered the mail until 1975. The *Miss America* was the first mail boat used by Captain Burnap who took the service over in 1929 and delivered mail until 1975. The boat was forty feet long with a cabin for mail and carried 17 passengers. A round trip from Old Forge to Inlet and back again was 75 cents. We decided to resurrect the *Miss America* under our Captain Conall McBride for our story!

Mail boat *Old Forge* on Fourth Lake. In 1903 the vessel delivered to 103 camps and hotels along the Fulton Chain.* Dave Beck collection. Courtesy Dave Beck.

Steamer *Clearwater* and mail boat *Old Forge*, Old Forge dock, 1920's. PC525 of TOWHA. Used with permission of Town of Webb Historical Association

While the historic mail boat operation has now ceased on First to Fourth Lakes along the Fulton Chain, mail boats do still operate on a few lakes in the region several months every year, including on Seventh Lake of the Fulton Chain, Raquette Lake and on Big Moose Lake which has the longest seasonal delivery time beginning in June and running until the end of September.

*For a comprehensive history of the mail boats along the Fulton Chain of Lakes, see Charles E. Herr's volume, *The Fulton Chain: Early Settlements, Roads, Steamboats, Railroads and Hotels*, HerrStory Publications, First Edition, May 2017, pp. 149–154.

Miss America delivering mail along the Fulton Chain of Lakes between Old Forge and Inlet, NY. From the author's collection

SPECIAL BONUS FEATURES

Photo © 2020 Gary VanRiper

The **White-throated Sparrow** is one of more than 200 bird species known to breed in the Adirondacks. The male has a beautiful song and has been called, Whistler of the North. This one was found in Ferd's Bog near Eagle Bay. Photo © 2020 Gary VanRiper

The **Black Bear** is one of nearly 60 species of mammals that reside in the Adirondack Park. We are often asked if we are afraid of bears. We certainly respect these powerful creatures, but are not fearful of them. This was a famous bear known around our small Adirondack community as 'Split Ear'. Photo © 2020 Gary VanRiper

Moss Lake in the west-central Adirondacks is one of more than 3000 lakes and ponds found in the 6 million-acre park. Justin prefers to paddle any time from dawn to early morning. Photo © 2020 Gary VanRiper

JACKIE SALSBERRY

- 12 years old
- 4'11" – 91.5 pounds
- Born and raised in the Adirondacks
- 1/4 Native American (on Mom's side)
- Summer house on 4th Lake island
- Strawberry blonde hair
- Brown eyes
- Highly Intelligent
- Athletic and Courageous
- Common Sense
- Organized, Perfectionist
- Greatest Fear: Spiders
- Favorite Book: *The Wizard of OZ*

NICK BARNES

- 10 years old
- 4'8" – 80 pounds
- 1/2 French Canadian (on Mom's side)
- 4-Season Camp on 4th Lake, Inlet, NY
- Boathouse built by great-grandfather
- Brown hair, Brown eyes
- Loves to eat
- Impulsive
- Likes being in charge (votes himself as mayor of Pioneer Village)
- Confuses meanings of words (i.e. vegetarian and veterinarian)
- Unlucky (especially with fishing gear)
- Greatest Fear: heights
- Reluctant Reader
- Favorite Book: *Treasure Island*

DAX
- 12 pounds
- Calico / Female
- Short hair / Green eyes
- Sleek and Athletic
- Brave and an Explorer
- Smart / Loyal
- Greatest Fear: predators

THE FULTON CHAIN
of Lakes
West-Central Adirondacks

MOSS LAKE

BUBB LAKE

SIS LAKE

4TH LAKE

ALGER ISLAND

BALD MOUNTAIN FIRE TOWER

SHOAL LIGHTHOUSE

BALD MOUNTAIN

3RD LAKE

2ND LAKE

OLD FORGE POND

1ST LAKE

CHANNEL

OLD FORGE

Dannemora

Saranac Lake

Jay

Lake Placid

Elizabethtown

Port Henry

Ticonderoga

NORTH CAROLINA

Stumpy Point

Kilkenny

Engelhard

Salvo

Pamlico Sound

Cranberry Lake

Star Lake

Spies on Castle Rock

Avon

Big Moose

Blue Mtn. Lake

Inlet

Old Forge

Hatteras

OUTER BANKS

Ocracoke

Atlantic Ocean

Adirondack Park

Speculator

Piseco

North Creek

Lake George

Northville

Caroga Lake

Where the Adirondack Kids® Stories Are Set

Share Our Good Nature

INLET

A Central Adirondack Community

Founded 1902

Photo © 2020 Gary VanRiper

Inlet, New York, in the west-central region of the Adirondack Park. Home of *The Adirondack Kids*® and epicenter for the book series.

Photo © 2020 Jim Payne, Payne's Air Service, Inlet, NY

THE STORY
Behind the Stories
Gary VanRiper

Have you ever been to the Adirondacks?

The amazing six-million-acre park in eastern New York state is so large you can fit several of America's national parks combined inside its borders!

Some 55 different species of mammals and more than 200 species of birds can be found living among the mountains, forests, lakes, streams and bogs within the Blue Line of the Park's massive wilderness.

Algonquin Peak is the second-highest mountain in the high peaks wilderness of the Adirondacks. In this research hike for The Adirondack Kids® #5, Justin's toes are pointed toward **Mount Colden** and the highest peak on the horizon is **Mount Marcy**.

Photo © 2020 Gary VanRiper

Our family has a camp that is more than 110 years old located in the west-central region of the park, so we know what the Adirondacks looks like, sounds like, smells like, feels like and even what it tastes like!

The real **Justin served as a model** for the character. Here you can see how this photograph was used by the artist on the **cover of the first book.** Photo ©2020 Gary VanRiper

When Justin was around nine-years-old, I knew he was fast approaching one of the danger times when young people are at risk of dropping out of reading for pleasure.

I had read aloud to him nearly every day of his life from the time he was an infant, but thought if we could write stories together it might help keep him interested in books and reading. It did! And the Adirondacks seemed the perfect place to set a story because we already knew it so well.

Detail by artist, Susan Loeffler, from the front cover of the original *Adirondack Kids* volume, number one. The reference photo (*opposite*) is the one she used for this section of the cover illustration.

The camp providing the initial inspiration for our stories has been in Carol's family for more than a century. Photo ©2020 Gary VanRiper

While growing up, the real Justin had quite a collection of **bucket hats**. That is why on nearly every cover of *The Adirondack Kids®* book series you see Justin, the character, wearing a different **bucket hat**! Photo © 2020 Gary VanRiper

Dax (short for, Adirondacks) has become one of the most popular characters in The Adirondack Kids® book series. We spelled her name, D-A-X, because we thought it looked cooler than, DACKS.

Photo ©2020 Gary VanRiper

Justin Robert is very much like the real Justin. They both wear bucket hats and like computers, peanut butter cups and animals – especially cats! And that is why we created the character, Dax. Over the years Dax has become one of our readers' favorite characters. We actually adopted the real Dax from a shelter and she became a model for our illustrators.

Unlike Justin, Jackie Salsberry and Nick Barnes were born entirely in our imaginations!

Virginia and Justin in a pose used by the illustrator in volume #16.

And yes, there is a real Pioneer Village and a *real* putt putt. That is Justin at the bow and Virginia steering the three cousins for Inlet, probably for ice cream. Virginia became the model for Jackie in our stories. Photos © 2020 Gary VanRiper

Carol VanRiper
Photo © 2020 Gary VanRiper

Carol VanRiper is my wife and Justin's mom. She and a very good friend of ours, Susan Loeffler, are among the artists that have brought our characters to life through their illustrations. Susan does all of our full-color work, and Carol, the black-and-white illustrations beginning with book number four of the series, *The Great Train Robbery.*

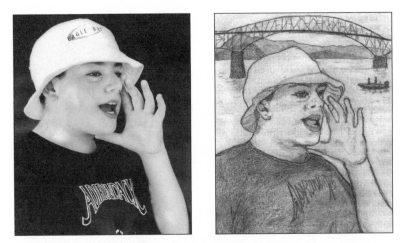

Do you like to draw? Here is an illustration Carol drew free-hand from the photo reference for The Adirondack Kids® #9: *Legend of the Lake Monster!* Susan Loeffler used the same photo for an illustration in The Adirondack Kids® Story & Coloring book, *Runaway Dax.* Perhaps one day you will be an illustrator, too! Photo © 2020 Gary VanRiper

The interior drawings for the first three books in the series were done by the talented Glenn Guy who was the political cartoonist for a community news-paper I co-owned those many years ago when the idea of publishing the first book was just a dream.

Photo © 2020 Carol VanRiper

Gary VanRiper

Susan Loeffler

We were encouraged, and became really serious about producing a complete manuscript, when a parent at a Parents As Reading Partners (PARP) event heard us read some of what we had written, and asked us when our book was coming out. A year later what began as a writing exercise at home blossomed into a chapter book, and eventually into a series and small family company.

Dax was right at home with her perch atop cases of The Adirondack Kids® adventure series. Here she is with our corporate logo.
Photo ©2020 Gary VanRiper

AKP

Our second **book signing** ever was at Borders in Syracuse, New York. Justin read a little from the book and we sold nearly 100 copies that day. Since then we have had the privilege of speaking at schools and libraries and conferences and conducting workshops on self-publishing throughout and around the **Adirondack Park.** Photo © 2020 Carol VanRiper

The Adirondack Kids® series of books is now approaching 175,000 copies sold, and we sincerely thank all the parents and grandparents and teachers and school administrators and librarians and bookstore owners who have believed in and supported our work throughout the past two decades.

One of the great privileges we have enjoyed over the years has been the opportunities to speak with students about reading and writing and exploring the great outdoors. Here we are autographing copies of *The Adirondack Kids* #1 for a One School – One Book program.
Photo © 2020 Carol VanRiper

Our first publicity shot taken by Carol at camp. Photo © 2020 Carol VanRiper

Our publicity shot today, taken at *Adirondack Kids Day™* in Inlet, NY. Photo © 2020 Jan Grzesik, Ltd.

And most of all, 'thank you' to our thousands of readers! Many of you, like Justin, are now grown and have started families of your own. As long as you keep on reading, we plan to keep on writing!

This is Levi Judah, the latest Adirondack kid in our family! Generation after generation passing on a love for books, reading and a deep appreciation of the environment. Photo © 2020 Justin VanRiper

WARNING

Reading *The Adirondack Kids®* book series may cause you to abandon your electronic devices to explore the great outdoors!

The Adirondack Kids® #1
When an uncommon pair of Common Loons takes up residence on the lake, three best friends (*The Adirondack Kids*) will do all they can to protect them.

The Adirondack Kids® #2
Rescue on Bald Mountain
One of *The Adirondack Kids* is afraid of heights and his two best friends think the way to help him overcome that fear is to climb a mountain.

The Adirondack Kids® #3
The Lost Lighthouse
When a sudden and violent storm chases *The Adirondack Kids* in their boat off the lake, they enter an unfamiliar forest that has harbored a secret for more than 100 years.

The Adirondack Kids® #4
The Great Train Robbery
The Adirondack Kids find themselves as reluctant detectives when a fake train robbery intended to be entertainment for tourists becomes the real thing.

The Adirondack Kids® #5
Islands in the Sky
(*1st place 2004–2005 for best children's book: Adirondack Center for Writing Literary Awards*). *The Adirondack Kids* are on a quest to summit their first Adirondack high peak. The pet cat of one of the kids is having her own unintended tour of the Adirondack Park.

The Adirondack Kids® #6
The Secret of the Skeleton Key
The discovery of a skeleton key in a bottle floating on the surface of the lake leads *The Adirondack Kids* to unlock an old camp mystery.

The Adirondack Kids® #7
Mystery of the Missing Moose
A local newspaper is offering a cash prize for a photograph of an elusive moose. *The Adirondack Kids* are led into a series of encounters with wildlife as they search to find it.

The Adirondack Kids® #8
Escape from Black Bear Mountain
The Adirondack Kids approach a harrowing scene involving what appears to be the serious plight of a young boy their age – yet things are not always what they seem to be!

The Adirondack Kids® #9
Legend of the Lake Monster
The Adirondack Kids seek an encounter with Champ – the 'Loch Ness Monster' of American folklore.

The Adirondack Kids® #10
The Final Daze of Summer
A 'Rare Bird Alert' causes *The Adirondack Kids* to investigate the waters and shoreline of the lake while avoiding what is also reportedly a prowling black bear.

The Adirondack Kids® #11
The Fall of Fort Ticonderoga
The Adirondack Kids inspire their community to produce a reenactment of Ethan Allen and the Green Mountain Boys and their capture of Fort Ticonderoga.

The Adirondack Kids® #12
The Pond Hockey Challenge
One of *The Adirondack Kids* volunteers her two inexperienced friends to join her in a pond hockey showdown with a powerful rival from a neighboring hamlet.

The Adirondack Kids® #13
The Carousel Case, The Bicycle Race & The Blackfly Bad Guy
Throughout the Adirondack Park there are reports of unique Black Fly artifacts gone missing. *The Adirondack Kids* solve the mystery.

The Adirondack Kids® #14
Journey into the Land of MakeBelieve
When *The Adirondack Kids* learn about a historic amusement park for children that was finally swept away by years of flooding, they decide to create their own.

The Adirondack Kids® #15
Mystery Under the Midnight Moon – A Collection of Short Stories
Five stories involving *The Adirondack Kids* in adventures including a missing cat, a lost ring, not-so-secret fears, maturing friendships and the introduction of a bright and inquisitive new character into the close-knit circle of friends.

The Adirondack Kids® #16
The Outlaws of Cascade Falls
The Adirondack Kids have heard there is an old safe abandoned somewhere along a trail in the deep woods and make it their mission to find it. What they don't expect to find are giant footprints ten times the size of their own.

The Adirondack Kids® #17
Spies on Castle Rock & the Secrets of the Secret Code
The Adirondack Kids form a team and plot a strategy to win a geocache competition that does not allow the use of any modern technology. It doesn't take them long to discover not everyone plays by the rules.

The Adirondack Kids® #18
Treasure in the Boathouse & the Misadventure of Nicholas T. Barnes
When it appears one of *The Adirondack Kids* may be moving, his friends are desperate to make plans for his final days in the Adirondack special. A stunning discovery in the attic of his boathouse could change everything.

The Adirondack Kids® #19
Phantom of the Talus Caves
How the familiar can appear strange when in unfamiliar territory! A bushwhack in search of a guide's legendary cave leads *The Adirondack Kids* to a surprising discovery. More than the cold can bring a chill in the night!

The Adirondack Kids® #20
The Amazing Migration Vacation
The Adirondack Kids are on vacation at what feels like the edge of the world! It's the Outer Banks of North Carolina. When meeting some Carolina kids surrounding a stranded bird familiar to them all, they discover there is a lot more they share in common.

www.ADIRONDACKKIDS.com

Also on sale wherever great books on the Adirondacks are found.

YouTube

Cast of Characters

THE ADIRONDACKS

- As old as the earth
- 6 million acres*
- Stunning beauty
- Striking wardrobe
- Demands respect
- Unpredictable
- Can be fickle
- Surprises the senses
- Has lots of secrets!
- Takes time to know

*Equal to combined size of
Yellowstone, Grand Canyon,
Yosemite, Everglades,
and Great Smoky Mountain
National Parks

Photo © 2020 Gary VanRiper

JUSTIN ROBERT

- 10 years old
- 4'6" – 72 pounds
- 4-Season Camp on 4th Lake, Inlet, NY
- Dark Brown hair
- Blue Eyes
- Likes peanut butter cups, computers, and riding his bike
- Loves the outdoors
- Loves animals – especially cats
- Thoughtful
- Peacemaker
- Greatest Fear: losing his friends
- Favorite Books: *Robin Hood* & *The Hobbit*